This Little Tiger book belongs to:

_____

_____

_____

To Donna, a winter's child, with love
~ K W

For my cousin Grace
~ A E

LITTLE TIGER PRESS
1 The Coda Centre, 189 Munster Road,
London SW6 6AW
www.littletigerpress.com

First published in Great Britain 2011
This edition published 2012

Text copyright © Kathryn White 2011
Illustrations copyright © Alison Edgson 2011
Kathryn White and Alison Edgson have asserted their rights to be
identified as the author and illustrator of this work under the
Copyright, Designs and Patents Act, 1988

A CIP catalogue record for this book is
available from the British Library

Printed in China • LTP/1400/0448/0512

2 4 6 8 10 9 7 5 3 1

When Will It Snow?

Kathryn White • Alison Edgson

LITTLE TIGER PRESS
London

"Winter is coming, Little Bear," Mother Bear
said. "Soon, icy winds will blow, bringing the
soft, white snow. We must snuggle down to
sleep, safe in our den."

"I don't want to sleep," said Little Bear.
"I want to play in the snow!"

Then he bounded away to hide.

"Oooh, I love hide-and-seek!" cried
Squirrel, peeping down from a tree.
"Sshhh!" Little Bear hushed.
"I'm not playing hide-and-seek.
I've run away."

Mole popped up from his burrow with a "Boo!"

So Little Bear stamped his foot, "I'm not playing, I'm hiding!"

"Why's that?" asked Squirrel.

"Because if I go home, I'll have to sleep for the whole winter. And I'll *never* know what snow is like."

"I'll show you what snow's like," chuckled Squirrel. "It just falls from the sky, like this." And she tossed some acorns into the air.

"Snow doesn't bounce like that!"
cried Mole. "Snow is soft and wet
– like this!"

He wiggled his bottom and
dived into a puddle. *Sploosh!*
Little Bear squealed with delight.

"Snow is thick," said Squirrel. "You can make snowmen with it and . . . SNOWBALLS!" And she tossed a ball of mud towards her friend.

Little Bear ducked but . . .

Splodge! The mud-ball soaked poor Mole!

"Snow is brilliant!" laughed Bear.
Suddenly there were mud-balls
flying everywhere.

"You can make angel wings in snow," said Squirrel, falling backwards and flapping her arms. When she stood up, there was an angel squirrel in the sand.

"I can do that too," whooped Little Bear as he and Mole joined in.

Soon angel wings scattered the ground.

Bear looked at his friends. "Will you two play in the snow while I'm asleep?" he asked.

"Oh yeah!" said Mole. "Hide-and-seek is great in the snow."

Just then, Little Bear heard his mother calling.
He flopped down in a huff.

"Grouchy grizzly!" giggled Mole, making
him a funny hat.

"Don't forget me," said Bear.

"'Course not!" said Squirrel.

But as Bear turned to take one last look at his friends, they were already playing without him.

"Us bears sleep through the winter," said Mother Bear softly. "And when we wake, the cold snow is gone."

"Will my friends be gone too?" whispered Little Bear.

"True friends are always there for you when you wake, like the blossom on the trees and the warm sunshine."

Then Mother Bear snuggled her little one gently into bed.

When Little Bear trudged back into his cave, Mother Bear reached out for a hug.

"I don't want hugs," said Bear. "I want to see the snow."

Outside the cave, the soft snow fell
all through the long winter.

Then one day, when the spring sunshine had melted the last of the snowflakes, Mother Bear gently shook Little Bear awake.

"Spring is here, little one," she said.

Bear raced out into the sunshine. The world was filled with the scent of blossom and fresh grass.

Bear ran straight to the muddy puddle to look for Squirrel and Mole. But they were nowhere to be seen.

"They've gone," he sighed. "They've forgotten all about me."

Just then, Little Bear heard a funny laugh. He quietly tiptoed through the trees . . .

There was Squirrel, dressed as a snowman!
"We've missed you, Bear," squealed Mole.
"Hide-and-seek isn't the same without you!"
Little Bear's eyes lit up. He had everything
he could wish for right in front of him – the
best friends in all the world.

Snuggle up

with these

cosy books

from

Little Tiger Press!

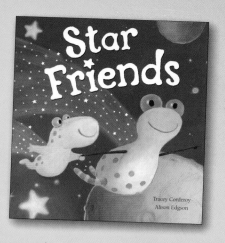

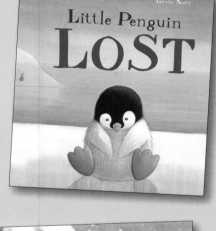

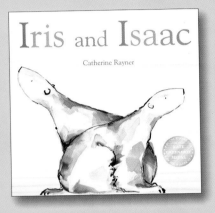

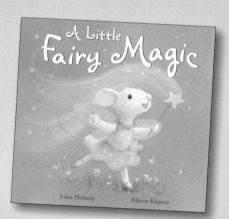

For information regarding any of the above titles
or for our catalogue, please contact us:
Little Tiger Press, 1 The Coda Centre,
189 Munster Road, London SW6 6AW
Tel: 020 7385 6333 • Fax: 020 7385 7333
E-mail: info@littletiger.co.uk
www.littletigerpress.com